MW00901743

Dilly the Dolphin

Short Stories, Games, and Jokes!

Uncle Amon

Copyright © 2016 Uncle Amon

All rights reserved. This book is a work of fiction. No part of this book or this book as a whole may be used, reproduced, or transmitted in any form without written permission from the author.

Published by Hey Sup Bye Publishing

ISBN-13: 978-1534958890
ISBN-10: 1534958894

TABLE OF CONTENTS

Dilly's First Day

It was Dilly the dolphin's first day at Freshwater Elementary School, and he was worried that he wouldn't have anything in common with the students there.

Dilly missed Saltwater Academy, where he used to go to school. He wished he had never agreed to be part of the exchange student program. At the time, it had sounded exciting to trade places with a river otter for a few months and find out what school was like for freshwater creatures. But now, Dilly wished he could make a different decision. He wondered if the river otter was feeling the same way.

His heart pounding rapidly, Dilly swam to Freshwater Elementary. School hadn't started yet, but the other students were already out front, playing hide-and-seek behind rocks and plants. The fish, turtles, otters, and ducks were very different from Dilly's old saltwater classmates. The plants were different, the rocks were different, and the water was very different.

What are all these river creatures going to think of someone like me? Dilly wondered. They've probably never even seen a dolphin before. I must seem as strange to them as they seem to me.

Just then, a friendly duckling happened to notice Dilly. "Hi!" she cried. "What's your name? Mine's Quackie."

Dilly stared at Quackie in shock. He had never talked to a duck before. He couldn't help but think how different Quackie was from the dolphins, whales, sea lions, and tropical fish back at Saltwater Academy.

"I'm Dilly," he said.

Quackie smiled. "Do you want to play hide-and-seek with us before school starts?"

Dilly looked at Quackie, then at the other creatures who would be his new classmates. They weren't anything like the friends he was used to.

"No, thanks," he said quietly.

"Why not?" chimed a turtle named Sheldon. "I'll help you find the best hiding places!"

Before Dilly could answer, the bell rang, and all the students swam into school. The classroom looked odd to Dilly, who was used to his tropical saltwater classroom back home. And the teacher, Ms. Beaver, was the strangest-looking, brown furry animal! Although she was nice to Dilly, he couldn't stop thinking how odd beavers were. In fact, everything here was odd!

All morning, Dilly felt like crying. How he longed to return to his home in the ocean. Freshwater life was too different for him to handle!

After lunch, the class had recess, and again they played outside. Dilly stayed close to the school and watched the others.

"Let's play Diving Dolphins!" Quackie suggested.

Dilly gasped. He and his friends at Saltwater Academy played Diving Dolphins all the time! He couldn't believe that these freshwater animals knew that such a game existed.

"Okay!" agreed Sheldon. "But Dilly has to join in. After all, who knows more about being a diving dolphin than he does?"

Quackie splashed over to Dilly. "Will you play with us?" she begged. "Please?"

Dilly thought about how friendly Quackie and the other river creatures had been. He thought about how welcoming Ms. Beaver had been. He also thought about his own attitude that morning. Was it possible that he hadn't been fair to his new school? After all, the river creatures were animals just like him, even if they were different from what Dilly was used to. They deserved for Dilly to give them a chance.

Dilly took a deep breath, smiled at Quackie, and said, "Sure!"

And, as he played Diving Dolphins with his new classmates, Dilly discovered that he and his freshwater friends were a lot more alike than he'd thought!

Freshwater Fun Day

"I'm so excited!" Quackie the duck bubbled. "Freshwater Fun Day is just around the corner!"

"Freshwater Fun Day?" Dilly repeated. "What's that?" Although Dilly had been attending Freshwater Elementary School for the past few weeks, there was a lot he still didn't know about river life. As an exchange student from Saltwater Academy, he was much more familiar with life in the ocean.

"You don't know about Freshwater Fun Day?" gasped Sheldon the turtle, another new friend of Dilly's. "It's only one of the best holidays of the year!"

"That's right!" agreed Quackie. "There's a huge river festival, with food and games and special programs. The river is decorated from bank to bank, and everyone dresses up, and all the animals and fish in the whole river celebrate what it means to be a freshwater creature!"

The moment Quackie finished speaking, she gasped. "That doesn't mean that saltwater creatures aren't invited," she quickly added.

"Of course it doesn't!" agreed Sheldon. "In fact, it'll be a great chance for you to learn more about freshwater life, Dilly!"

Dilly had to agree that Freshwater Fun Day sounded interesting. But he couldn't help feeling a wave of homesickness for the ocean, where everyone was now getting ready to celebrate Salty Seas Day.

Just the same, Dilly celebrated Freshwater Fun Day with Quackie, Sheldon, and the rest of his new schoolmates. The festival was just as wonderful as Quackie had said, and Dilly enjoyed the freshwater food and the freshwater games and the big display of fireworks over the river at night.

Still, he couldn't help but feel a little lonely. Freshwater Fun Day was a tradition for everyone else in the river. But, for Dilly, it was something brand-new.

On Monday at school, Ms. Beaver talked with her class about the recent holiday. "I want you all to write a short report about Freshwater Fun Day," she said. "You can write about the holiday's history, or you can write about a special tradition that you enjoy."

"And Dilly," she went on, "you are certainly welcome to write about Freshwater Fun Day, but I thought you might enjoy writing a report about Salty Seas Day instead. Then you could read it to our class, and we could all learn about a saltwater holiday."

Dilly was thrilled with that idea! He went right home and whipped up the best report he had ever written. But he didn't stop there. He spent the rest of the afternoon cooking and working at his craft table.

The next day, Dilly proudly read his report to his freshwater classmates. He was pleased that they seemed so fascinated by his description of Salty Seas Day.

"We dance to tropical music and eat tropical food and give each other brightly-colored cards," Dilly read. "Saltwater Seas Day is all about how special it is to be a saltwater creature!"

After he was finished, Dilly passed around the sushi he had made yesterday. Then he gave each of his classmates a colorful card and a tropical flower necklace to wear. Quackie, Sheldon, and all the others oohed and aahed.

"This sushi is delicious, Dilly!" cried Ms. Beaver.

"Let's put on some tropical music and dance!" suggested Quackie. So they did.

Dilly couldn't remember a time when he'd felt prouder. Just as his new classmates had shared their holiday with him, now he was sharing his holiday with them.

I sure am learning a lot, thought Dilly, and so are they!

In fact, it may have been the very best Salty Seas Day that Dilly had ever celebrated!

Just for Fun Activity

Ask an adult to help you look up facts about a holiday that is celebrated in a culture different from yours. Then, plan a party to celebrate that holiday and invite a few friends over! You can serve some of the food that is eaten on that holiday, make appropriate decorations, and read books, play games, or watch videos related to the holiday. This is a great way to learn about other cultures and customs. It's also very fun!

Dilly Meets Tippy the Toad

One morning, Dilly the dolphin happily swam into his classroom at Freshwater Elementary. He stopped in surprise when he noticed a new student in the room.

As class began, Dilly's teacher Ms. Beaver introduced the new student as Tippy the toad. "Tippy just moved here from downriver," she explained. "Please do your best to make her feel welcome."

Tippy looked around at the class before taking her seat. When she saw Dilly, she gave him a strange look. But Dilly decided that maybe he'd imagined it, and he made up his mind to help Tippy feel at home. After all, his freshwater classmates had been kind and welcoming to him when he was a brand-new exchange student. He knew just how Tippy felt.

At recess, Dilly and his friends Quackie the duck and Sheldon the turtle decided to ask Tippy to play with them.

"Do you want to join us in a game of river tag?" Sheldon asked her.

"That depends on who's going to play," replied Tippy.

"Quackie and Dilly and I," said Sheldon, motioning at his friends.

Tippy gave Dilly another strange look. Then she turned away and hopped onto a rock to sit in the sun. "I think I'd rather not," she told Sheldon.

"What was that all about?" Sheldon whispered to his friends.

Dilly had a very bad feeling that he knew. "I don't think Tippy likes me," he said slowly.

"But she doesn't even know you!" cried Quackie.

"She doesn't have to know me," Dilly explained. "She made up her mind not to like me just because I'm different. I'm not a freshwater creature like the rest of you."

"So, why does that matter?" Quackie cried, putting her wings on her hips.

Dilly thought back to his first day at Freshwater Elementary. At first, he had felt uncomfortable around his freshwater classmates just because they were different. Luckily, he had quickly figured out that it was silly to think like that, and before long, he had made some great friends.

Now, it looked like Tippy needed to learn that same lesson. Dilly remembered that he had finally begun to feel comfortable when his new classmates suggested playing one of his favorite games. If Dilly found something that he and Tippy had in common, maybe Tippy would decide to give him a chance, too!

Suddenly, Dilly had a great idea. He turned to his friends and began talking loudly. "I can't wait to get home from school and watch *Terrific Toads* this afternoon," he said, naming a new TV show that he enjoyed.

"Those toads sure are clever!" Quackie agreed, catching on.

"And so talented!" added Sheldon.

Sure enough, Dilly had caught Tippy's attention. "You watch *Terrific Toads*?" she asked. "So do I! It's my favorite show! I didn't think saltwater animals cared about freshwater shows."

"Are you kidding?" asked Dilly. "After all, we all live in the water. And those toads are pretty amazing!"

For the first time, Tippy smiled at Dilly. "I don't know if you noticed," she said, "but I was kind of rude to you today. I'd never met a saltwater animal before, and I was afraid you wouldn't like me. But I guess I was wrong. Will you forgive me?"

"Of course!" Dilly replied, grinning at Quackie and Sheldon. "But you have to do one thing, Tippy."

"What's that?" Tippy asked.

"You have to play river tag with us!" Dilly answered.

Tippy giggled. "It's a deal!"

And, from that day on, Dilly, Tippy, Quackie, and Sheldon were the very best of friends.

Field Day Celebrations

Dilly the dolphin was very excited when his teacher, Ms. Beaver, told her class that Freshwater Elementary School's field day was coming up. Dilly remembered field day at his old school, Saltwater Academy. Last year, he had won first-place ribbons for water-spouting and jumping through hoops, two things that dolphins are great at. Dilly hoped he would bring home more blue ribbons from Freshwater Elementary!

Field day dawned clear and bright, and Ms. Beaver took her class upriver, where there was more room to compete.

Dilly's heart danced with excitement. He could hardly wait to get started.

But field day at Freshwater Elementary didn't start out like Dilly had expected. First, Ms. Beaver announced a lily-pad race. The contestants had to jump from lily pad to lily pad across the width of the river. Whoever made it to the other side first was the winner. Tippy the toad won that race. Dilly, who was too big to fit on a lily pad, touched each of them with his nose as he swam, but he still came in last.

Next, it was time for the diving competition. Ms. Beaver tossed some polished pebbles to the bottom of the river and told her students that whoever was the first to come back to the surface with a pebble was the winner.

Dilly considered himself a pretty good diver, but he quickly found that diving in a river was not at all like diving in the ocean. It was too murky and dark in the river for him to see clearly. By the time Dilly found a pebble and returned to the surface, he found that he was in last place—again. His friend, Quackie the duck, had won that competition.

By the third event, Dilly was beginning to feel rather discouraged. The third event was the backstroke race, and two of Dilly's river otter classmates tied. Otters were expert at swimming on their backs.

As the day continued, Dilly realized that he wasn't having any fun at all. He did poorly at all of the events. Freshwater Elementary's field day was just like it sounded—a field day for freshwater animals! As a saltwater animal, Dilly was just no good at any of the events.

When the class took a break for lunch, Quackie noticed that Dilly was sad.

"What's wrong?" Quackie asked him.

Dilly sighed. "All these events are freshwater events," he said, "and I can't do any of them!" Then he told her about Saltwater Academy's field day and the blue ribbons he had won.

That gave Quackie an idea.

When Dilly wasn't looking, Quackie swam over to Ms. Beaver and whispered in her ear.

Ms. Beaver smiled and nodded. "Class," she announced, "our next event will be…the hoop-jumping competition!"

Dilly hadn't been that surprised in a long time! And, although his classmates did their best to compete against him, he won the blue ribbon for hoop-jumping!

"Thanks for giving Ms. Beaver the idea for that event," Dilly told Quackie. "It was nice to do well at something—even if it wasn't a freshwater event!"

Quackie grinned. "So what if it wasn't a freshwater event? We may be different, but we've all got special talents—and yours is definitely hoop-jumping!"

That night, Dilly went to bed a happy dolphin—with his blue ribbon tucked beneath his fin.

Just for Fun Activity

If it's rainy out and you're stuck inside, why not have your own rainy day field day with your friends or siblings? Create some indoor events—sit-up competitions, mini-marshmallow-eating contests, bean-bag tosses, the sky's the limit! Don't forget: it's not always about winning - it's all about the fun!

Welcome Back, Dilly!

Dilly the dolphin knew he was going to miss Freshwater Elementary School. After spending half the school year with his new friends in the river, Dilly had learned a lot about freshwater life, and he had even begun to feel at home. But Dilly's real home was in the ocean, and since he was an exchange student, it was time for him to return to Saltwater Academy.

On Dilly's last day at Freshwater Elementary, his teacher Ms. Beaver and all of his classmates threw him a surprise party, complete with snacks and presents.

"We're going to miss you, Dilly!" his friend Quackie the duck told him.

"School won't be the same without you," Sheldon the turtle added.

"Promise you'll keep in touch by writing letters—and coming to visit as often as you can!" chimed Tippy the toad.

"I promise," said Dilly, his eyes filling with tears.

When school was over for the day, Quackie, Sheldon, and Tippy went home with Dilly to help him pack for his return to the ocean. They all shared a long, sad goodbye—and then Dilly was on his way. Already, he couldn't wait to come back to the river for a visit with his friends!

Although Dilly was very sad about leaving his freshwater friends, he began to feel excited as he entered the ocean once more. The colorful, tropical surroundings seemed especially bright and beautiful to him, and he realized how much he had missed his home.

When he reached the cave where he lived, Dilly smiled at the sight of his cozy bed, his seashell decorations, and the seaweed plants that grew by his door.

"Welcome home, Dilly!" a chorus of voices called out, and Dilly spun in surprise to see his old friends Wanda the whale, Slipper the sea lion, and Aqua the fish.

"I missed you guys so much!" Dilly cried. "It's so good to see you!"

"We missed you, too!" Wanda told him. "Everyone at school is going to be so excited to see you tomorrow!"

Sure enough, the next day at school, Dilly was crowded by his friends and classmates, who were full of questions about what it was like to go to school with freshwater animals.

Finally, Dilly's old teacher, Mr. Seagull, had to calm the class down. "Why don't we have Dilly come to the front of the classroom and tell us about his time at Freshwater Elementary so that everyone can hear?"

Dilly swam to the front of the class and cleared his throat. "At first, I was nervous about starting at Freshwater Elementary," he began. "It was scary being in a new place, and I wasn't sure I was going to be comfortable around the freshwater animals."

"What were the freshwater animals like?" a tropical fish called out. "Very different from us, right?"

Dilly smiled. "Actually," he said, "that's what I thought at first. But it didn't take me long to realize that no matter who we are or where we live, we're all the same on the inside. I had a lot of fun learning about the differences between saltwater animals and freshwater ones—but I had even more fun learning about how much we all have in common!"

"Well said, Dilly," Mr. Seagull told him. "It sounds like you had a wonderful experience."

"Oh, I sure did," replied Dilly. He looked at his Saltwater Academy classmates. He thought about his Freshwater Elementary classmates. He was such a lucky dolphin to have two amazing sets of friends.

Dilly the dolphin really did have the best of both worlds!

Funny Jokes

Q: Why are fish so gullible?

A: They always fall for the hook, line, and sinker!

Q: Which fish dresses the best?

A: The swordfish because he always looks sharp!

Q: Why are fish shoes the warmest ones to wear?

A: They have electric eels!

Q: Where do fish come from?

A: Finland!

Q: How do you communicate with a fish?

A: Drop it a line!

Q: Why should you use six hooks on your fishing line?

A: It would be more eFISHient!

Q: What kind of revenue do fishermen make?

A: Net profits!

Q: How do fish run a business?

A: The start on a small scale!

Q: Why didn't Noah fish much while on the ark?

A: He only had two worms!

Q: Which fish only swims at night?

A: Starfish!

Q: How do the fish get to school?

A: On an octobus!

Q: Where do fish go to borrow money?

A: A loan shark!

Q: Where do fish bathe?

A: In the river basin!

Q: Why is a fish easy to weigh?

A: It has its own scales!

Q: What fish is best to have in a boat?

A: A sailfish!

Q: Why are fish bad at tennis?

A: They don't like to get close to the net!

Q: What fish makes the best sandwiches?

A: The peanut butter and jellyfish!

Q: What is a sea serpent's favorite meal?

A: Fish and ships!

Q: Which fish go to heaven when they die?

A: Angelfish!

Q: Where do fish usually sleep?

A: In a riverbed!

Q: What is a knight's favorite fish?

A: Swordfish!

Q: Why are fish so smart?

A: They are always in a school!

How Many?

Find the Differences

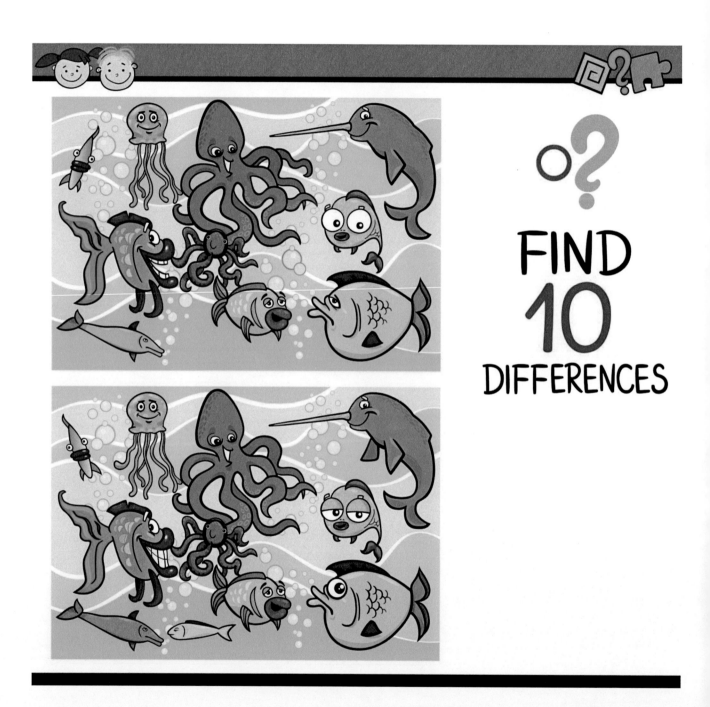

FIND
10
DIFFERENCES

Maze #1

Maze #2

Maze #3

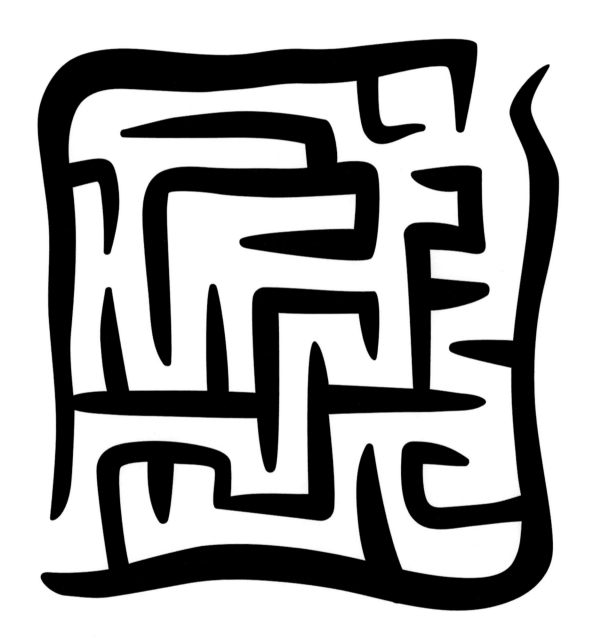

Game and Puzzle Solutions

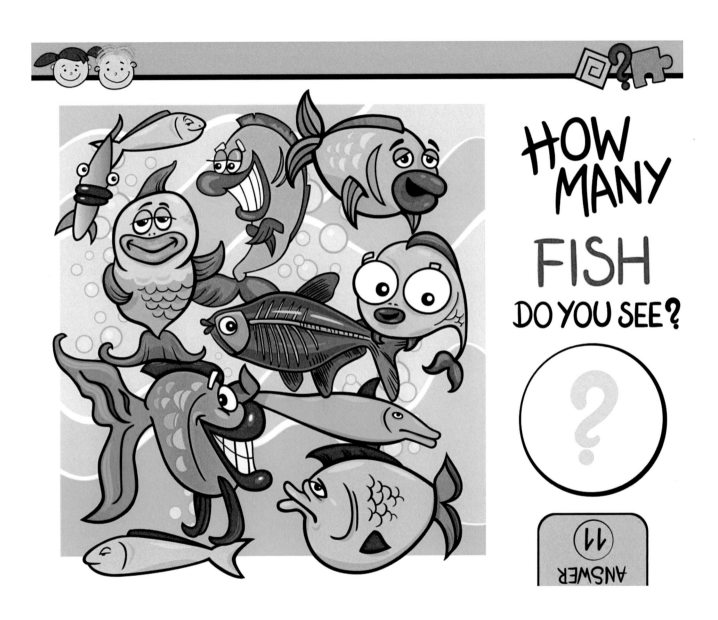

FIND
10
DIFFERENCES

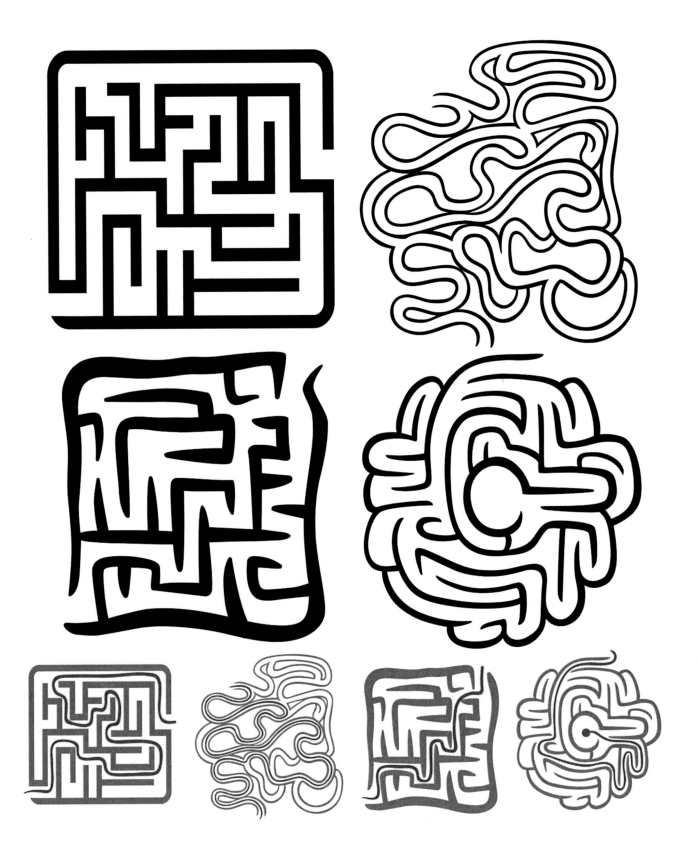

ABOUT THE AUTHOR

Uncle Amon began his career with a vision. It was to influence and create a positive change in the world through children's books by sharing fun and inspiring stories. Whether it is an important lesson or just creating laughs, Uncle Amon provides insightful stories that are sure to bring a smile to your face! His unique style and creativity stand out from other children's book authors, because he uses real life experiences to tell a tale of imagination and adventure.

"I always shoot for the moon. And if I miss? I'll land in the stars."
-Uncle Amon

Copyright © 2016 Uncle Amon Books. All rights reserved. This book is a work of fiction. No part of this book or this book as a whole may be used, reproduced, or transmitted in any form or means without written permission from the publisher. Graphics and images used in this book are licensed and © Dollar Photo Club

76962715R00022

Made in the USA
San Bernardino, CA
17 May 2018